SNOWDROP

The Spikeshuffler

Never judge anyone just because they're different…

Best Wishes

Peter Banc

A catalogue record for this book is available from the British Library

First Edition 2017
First published in Great Britain in 2017 by Pro-Actif Communications

Written by: Peter Barron
Illustrated by: Jonathan Raiseborough

Printed in EU by www.pulsioprint.co.uk

ISBN: 978-1-908211-63-7

2

FOREWORD

This book is aimed at helping children - and adults for that matter - to understand why prejudice is hurtful and needs to be overcome.

It has been published with the generous support of the North East Autism Society.

The background to how that support came about can be found at the end of the story, in the details about the illustrator and the author.

Snowdrop The Spikeshuffler is dedicated to anyone who has ever been judged because, in the eyes of others, they were different.

**north east
autism society**

CONTENTS

CHAPTER ONE

FREAK OF NATURE

SNOWDROP

HE was different from the very beginning. From the moment he came into the world in the warm, cosy nest beneath the old hedgerow, the difference couldn't be hidden. And, as a result, it seemed that his stay on earth was destined to be brief.

"It doesn't matter – he's still our son," Twig Hawthorn whispered, soothingly, to his wife, Poppy, as they looked down at their five new

babies which had been born as the first stabs of sunrise broke through the branches.

"But they'll take him away," gasped Poppy. "I know they will. They'll kill him because he's… because he's different."

"No they won't! Never!" declared Twig, his words slow but rising with defiance. "He's more than different. He's special."

The other Hawthorn youngsters, three males and a female, were ordinary, healthy, hungry, hedgehogs – or spikeshufflers as they were known in Merlin's Meadow. But the fifth youngster was pure white. He was the first albino spikeshuffler to be born in living memory.

"We could call him Snowdrop," suggested Twig. Poppy managed a smile in agreement and nuzzled her dear husband.

SNOWDROP

The Hawthorns were a long-established and well-respected spikeshuffler family in the meadow, which sheltered beneath Nab Top Mountain with its crooked peak, like an old witch's nose. There had been troubles to overcome before. There was the day of fire, seven summers past, when the flames skipped across the tinder-dry meadow at the speed of frightened rabbits, reducing the vibrant grasses to a black desert, reeking of acrid smoke. And there was still talk of the angry waters, when it rained for weeks and the streams and rivers turned the valley into a sea of death. But never in their history had the Hawthorns faced such a crisis on their own. And Poppy was right. They did try to take him.

Just as the Hawthorns had feared, a delegation from the High Council arrived at the hedgerow within a day of the birth. Following an untimely visit by an inquisitive dormouse, or furtail as they were known, the news had spread across the meadow as quickly as the flames in the great fire.

Very soon, every creature for miles around knew that a white spikeshuffler – "a freak of nature" – had been born.

"I'm sorry but there is no other way," insisted Peat Blackthorn, the stern-faced leader of the Council of Spikeshufflers, as a lone raven hovered overhead. "A white spikeshuffler will bring bad luck to the entire meadow," he declared.

Dropping the tone of his voice slightly at the sight of Poppy's tears, Peat tried to reason: "Look, he has nothing to hide him. He won't last a single day in the wild. You know what the scavengers are like – they'll take him and rip his body apart. It would be kinder to drown him in The Great Pond before he comes to know the fullness of life."

Poppy whimpered at the thought and tugged little Snowdrop to her side as Peat and the guards edged closer. Twig's spikes bristled as he faced up to the council leader and mustered the most passionate speech of his life:

"Over my own dead body," he began. "Can you not hear what you are saying? Why should his colour matter? Are we not all the same inside? Do we not have the same colour blood running through our bodies? Must we reject something just because it is different? This is my son. He's a Hawthorn and he stays. He will learn to survive – I will teach him."

Freak of nature

Standing at the front of a triangle of guards, Peat glared back at Twig in silence. For perhaps a minute, it seemed that he might choose to assert his authority and fight. He had known Twig for many seasons and knew him to be stout-hearted and devoted to his family. For that, he deserved respect. He would put up a valiant struggle, Peat knew there was no doubt about that, but he would quickly be overpowered by the guards. There was a further silence before Peat grunted. His head said that force was necessary to achieve what must be done, but his heart was heavy and it held sway.

"Let this be on your head, Twig," he said, quietly.

"No, Leader," cried one of the guards, a headstrong young spikeshuffler named Flint Featherstone. "This is wrong – you know it's wrong."

"Wrong! Wrong! Wrong!" chanted the other guards. "Kill him. Kill him."

"Enough!" demanded Peat.

He turned and the delegation shuffled away, chuntering between themselves, and leaving a dark cloud of prejudice hanging across Merlin's Meadow.

The sadness was that other spikeshufflers went on to forbid their young ones to have anything to do with "the white freak with unpure blood". They were ordered to avoid going near the Hawthorn's hedgerow. Even touching him would bring the most terrible misfortune. The flames or the angry waters would surely return.

But Twig Hawthorn's instincts were well-founded. Snowdrop wasn't just different. He was special – in his heart and in his blood.

CHAPTER TWO

A TEST OF SURVIVAL

SNOWDROP

AT first, Snowdrop Hawthorn found it hard to love himself. He didn't understand why he was so hated, why other spikeshufflers looked the other way, but he believed deep down it had to be his fault. Although he was white from the tip of his nose to his feet, he somehow felt dirty.

One morning, when the air was still enough to ensure there would be no ripples, Twig took

A test of survival

Snowdrop to The Great Pond and told him to look down from the grassy bank into the water.

"It is only ignorance – the fear of what they don't understand," explained Twig, solemnly. "You see, you were born different from any other spikeshuffler in Merlin's Meadow. You are the colour of snow and I am the colour of the earth. That makes you special but it also makes you vulnerable and that's why we must work extra hard to protect you."

Snowdrop watched his reflection staring back and a single tear sent his white outline shimmering in circles across to the middle of the pond, where a razor-toothed pike leapt at a fat dragonfly and shattered the picture completely.

"Why did I have to be different? Why couldn't I be just like the others?" he said, almost to himself.

SNOWDROP

He sensed that one day, he would have to make his own way in the world, without his mother and father. It was the way with all animals, but not just yet. It took time and love and patience, but Snowdrop gradually came to terms with who he was, what he looked like, and he learned to accept the way he was treated by those who knew no better. There was so much to learn and he couldn't be lonely, not with three brothers and a sister to play with and snuggle up to.

In the early days, he was not allowed to venture away from the nest. Like the others, he was taught to catch grubs, slugs and even small mice that strayed too close. They were warm, blissfully happy days, burying himself into his mother's side whenever he felt the need. Sometimes, it was an unexpected sound or smell that sent him scurrying to her. But often, it was just because she was there and he needed to be close to her. When night fell, she would tell him stories about the world beyond the meadow, and show him how to trace the shapes of animals in the stars that pricked the vast black blanket covering the meadow. He loved her as much as he could imagine but, as the weeks passed, and he grew stronger, he began to be less dependent on his mother and spend more time with his father. He was allowed to wander further afield, as long as Twig was with him, guiding him in the ways of the meadow, instilling in him the need to respect all living things, even those it was necessary to eat.

The bond between father and son grew stronger with each day, much more than with the other

SNOWDROP

Hawthorn youngsters. Twig loved them all, of course, but he knew that Snowdrop would need extra help if he were to make his way in the world. They became as close as the bark around a tree, venturing through the trails of the meadow, exploring so much that was new: the dazzling green foliage with its never-ending array of bugs and butterflies; and the sunbeams that bounced off the shimmering leaves, carrying the sounds of the birds down to the earth.

Snowdrop learned the importance of rolling in the loose undergrowth so that grass and bits of wood stuck to his spikes, providing priceless camouflage. At first, he thought he would never be able to flip himself over onto his back. It wasn't natural and it was exhausting. But Twig urged him on and, eventually, he found himself upside down and looking up at the sky – the fantastic, mesmerising sky which went on for ever and ever. Before long, he could flip over and back again at will, then roll himself into a ball so tight that he was half his normal size.

The test came when they heard the sound of The Whistler approaching through the crunchy grass. He was a human who frequently came to the river to catch fish with a strange, long stick-thing, and he always whistled, like a giant, happy bird. He came within feet of the two rolled-up spikeshufflers but his enormous, mud-caked boots kept striding past and the whistling faded, tunefully, into the distance.

It showed that Snowdrop was almost ready. Rooting out food and rolling into a camouflaged ball were things that Twig could teach his son.

SNOWDROP

But there was something else, something that would be key to his son's survival, that could not be taught because it was a gift he had been born with. It first came to light when a startled hare clattered clumsily out of a copse, bouncing high into the air in a mad panic, then streaking across the meadow as if its tail were on fire. To Twig's amazement, Snowdrop started running too – in the opposite direction. Well, it was an awkward kind of scuttling, really, with his bottom wiggling as he went, but it was running nonetheless.

Spikeshufflers don't run very fast. They're not built for it. But Snowdrop was special. His father had always said it, and it was true. Not only could he run, but he could run pretty fast – not as speedy as a hare, of course, but quick enough to be unique in the history of spikeshufflers.

CHAPTER THREE

ALONE IN THE WORLD

SNOWDROP

TIME was running quickly too. Twig knew that the day he dreaded – the day of separation – was coming soon. He and Poppy had discussed it. It was simply the way of the meadow. Sooner or later, creatures must become independent.

"It's time, my dear," said Twig, snuggling up to Poppy. "It's time to let him go now."

Poppy whimpered, like she had whimpered on the day the guards first came, but she knew there was no other way. That night, she slept close to Snowdrop, licking his head, gently, as he slept, wondering what might be his future, and knowing she may never see him again.

"Goodbye, my son," she whispered as Twig and Snowdrop set out the next morning. "Goodbye, my sweet Snowdrop."

The best way was for it to come without

warning. At the end of another glorious day
of exploration and wonder by his father's side,
Snowdrop turned round to discover that he
was alone.

SNOWDROP

"Father. Father, where are you?" he called, but
there was no answer. The meadow was suddenly
darker, emptier and colder. As if in respectful
recognition of the parting, the birds stopped
singing and the insects stopped flitting and
buzzing. At least, that's the way it seemed to
Snowdrop. For a while, an hour perhaps, Twig
watched secretly from the undergrowth, just in
case. Somehow, he managed to resist the
haunting calls of "Father, Father" which grew
louder until they reached a peak and then faded
into a soft whimpering and eventual silence.
Tearing himself away was the hardest thing
Twig had ever had to do but, finally, he forced
himself to begin the long walk back to the nest
to be with Poppy.

For days, Snowdrop continued the vain search for his father. He wandered, helplessly, by day and cried himself to sleep at night. At first, he feared something terrible had happened: that Twig had been taken by an enemy in a silent, split-second swoop. He searched everywhere but, deep down, there was an instinct, a knowledge, telling him that this was how it had to be.

Through a combination of luck and judgement, Snowdrop did survive, though there were many close shaves along the way. The first came in the earliest days of his time alone and resulted, again, from prejudice. He'd slept in a thick patch of foxgloves which had grown around the trunk of a tree. Woken by hunger, Snowdrop nudged his way into the watery early morning light and was immediately confronted by a pair of eyes, then another, then another. He shuffled backwards slightly as it became clear that six young spikeshufflers, around his own age, were standing in his way, their spikes standing to attention.

"Good morning, freak," said the closest of the gang, all of whom had their faces caked in dark green moss. "We all thought – hoped – you'd be dead by now. What's it like to be different and alone?"

Snowdrop said nothing, but tensed as he realised four more spikeshufflers had sneaked up behind him, flattening paths through the foxgloves.

"What do you want with me?" asked Snowdrop. "I mean no-one any harm."

"It's simple," said the gang leader. "There must

be no unpure bloods amongst the spikeshufflers in the meadow."

Without another word, the circle of spikeshufflers closed in on Snowdrop, all ten of them, their eyes blazing with ignorance and hate.

For a second, Snowdrop stood still, bewildered at the actions of his own kind. Why were they like this? Why were their faces painted so hideously?

As they came in closer, Snowdrop saw a gap in their ranks, ran for it and, with tears of despair falling as he went, didn't look back. If he had, he would have seen the expressions of disbelief on the faces of his tormentors who had never dreamed that a spikeshuffler could move so fast. He was gone from them in a white blur.

SNOWDROP

The narrowest escape of all came five or six sunrises later. Snowdrop was walking down a mossy track, still hoping against hope that his father would appear, when he heard a sudden, blood-curdling shriek. Schemer, the weasel – or slybody as they were known in the meadow – landed in front of him, with his needle-sharp

teeth bared. Snowdrop had been taught to roll up into a ball when faced with danger but he was definitely different. Instinctively, he began to run, the pace matching the rapid beat of his heart. Fear surged through his body, forcing him on, as he pelted blindly through the thick grasses and leaves of the meadow. But even the fastest spikeshuffler in history couldn't outrun a slybody. Schemer had initially been taken by surprise. He had never come across a white spikeshuffler, let alone one that could run, although he had heard about the birth of the freak. A second or two passed before he gave chase – seconds that would never have normally been afforded to any prey – and he chuckled as he torpedoed through the undergrowth, amused by the very thought of a spikeshuffler which

could move so fast. Despite it all, he caught
Snowdrop with relative ease, leapt onto the
spikeshuffler's back, and used his claws to pull
him to a shuddering halt. Snowdrop found
himself being dragged onto his back and saw the
terrifying flash of white as Schemer prepared to
sink his teeth into the flesh of his underbelly.

Snowdrop was ready for death. He looked up at
the blue sky overhead and closed his eyes,
waiting for the kill. Instead of the dagger of pain
he expected, he felt a strange, floating sensation
and a rushing of wind all around him. His
stomach was turning inside out but he dare not
open his eyes in case death was too terrible to
see. He felt his body rise, and there was a
short-lived dizziness and sickness, but still he
did not look.

Finally, there was a serene sense of peace amid the self-imposed blackness and he was sure it was over. One at a time, he half opened his eyes. The world was shimmering green. He opened his eyes fully and the light poured in, making it impossible to focus for a few seconds. Gradually, the world became sharper at the edges. He wasn't dead, or at least he didn't think so. He was standing in a clump of ferns, with the sunlight spearing through the gaps. Schemer was nowhere to be seen – and Snowdrop was alive.

CHAPTER FOUR

THE WINDSEEKER

SNOWDROP

THE four-leaf clover, sprouting amid an explosion of daisies, moved so slightly that it might easily have been the result of the faintest breath of wind. Only Godric, the old eagle, or windseeker, would have noticed as he arced effortlessly and silently overhead.

There it was again. Breeze or breakfast? Godric's eyes were locked on the movement like a heat-seeking missile locks on to an enemy plane.

"A nice juicy furtail for starters perhaps before I pluck a delicious greyflapper from the river a little later," he mused to himself, contentedly.

 The eye in the sky never blinked as a white snout disturbed the dew, collecting a droplet as it poked out and

sniffed the morning air. A pair of pink beady
eyes, like redcurrants, followed and only then did
Godric relax every sinew.

"Mmm. It's only the white spikeshuffler,"
he sighed, disappointed in one way but quite
pleased in another.

SNOWDROP

Four seasons had passed – a long time in the life of a spikeshuffler – and Snowdrop had continued to survive. More than that, he had earned a grudging respect across the meadow because he had lived when all around him expected him to die, although the other spikeshufflers still kept their distance. Today, he was out for an early poke around. He was always the first to emerge in the morning. Life was too short for sleeping – there was too much to explore.

Godric didn't eat spikeshufflers. They were far too prickly, unlike furtails (field-mice) and greyflappers (rainbow trout) from the river, his preferred courses. Spikeshufflers really weren't worth the trouble. And if you couldn't eat them, you might as well get to know them. He and

Snowdrop weren't exactly best friends.
Snowdrop had suggested it once but Godric had
insisted it simply wasn't possible.

"The space between the ground and the sky
is too great for spikeshufflers and windseekers
to become close," Godric had declared,
a little pompously.

But he was prepared to accept that the white
spikeshuffler was out of the ordinary and he'd
grown to quite like him since the day he'd saved
him from the slybody. He didn't really know why
he'd done that. It was probably as much his
dislike for Schemer, and all slybodies, as his
compassion for Snowdrop that had stirred him
into action. He'd swooped down and plucked up
the spikeshuffler in his talons just as the weasel
was about to kill him. The old eagle had been

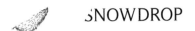

to watch the young spikeshuffler's prog... ever since. He would perch on a branch or fence and pass the time of day with the young spikeshuffler, discussing the weather, and local animal gossip such as the birth of a new litter of fox cubs, the death of an ancient badger, or the latest weasel fight.

"Did you hear the screams? The slybodies were fighting again last night," Snowdrop would report.

"It's time they were banned from the meadow," Godric would invariably declare.

More than anything, the little white spikeshuffler loved to talk to the windseeker about flying. The idea of soaring on the wind, hovering one minute and diving the next, fascinated him and filled him with longing.

The Windseeker

"What's it like to be a windseeker? Does it take long to learn? Is it hard to hover? How do you glide without moving your wings?"

The questions always came thick and fast and Godric basked in the attention. If only the spikeshuffler knew. Gliding might look effortless but every muscle in the wings was working hard to play its part. To Snowdrop, flying represented freedom – a new world. It made his four stumpy little legs seem totally inadequate, even if they could carry him faster than any other spikeshuffler. They were so short, he couldn't even see over a dockleaf patch. Even the nose-twitchers (rabbits) could jump high enough to see over a dockleaf patch.

Godric, in contrast, could see everything and Snowdrop had a recurring dream in which his

legs turned into wings and he could fly like
a windseeker.

As Snowdrop emerged from the clump of
daisies, an enticing smell reached his nostrils.
The aroma came from across the road which had
bisected the animals' world two winters past.

"Biscuits," he whispered to himself. "Food of
the Gods."

Ethel Gibbons, the old lady who had refused to
sell up when the road-builders moved in, often
brought fresh water and tidbits across to the edge
of the meadow for the wild creatures. This time,
she'd left a big plateful of home-made ginger
biscuits outside her cottage door to entice Smarty
Pants, her beloved ginger cat, back home after a
night out. Newly-baked biscuits was a scent
Snowdrop couldn't resist, even though it meant

crossing the great concrete river. It was as though an invisible thread was tied to his nose and was pulling him, irresistibly, in the direction of crumbly biscuit heaven. Up above, the all-seeing Godric cried out a warning but it was lost in Snowdrop's fog of desire.

CHAPTER FIVE

THE FLYMAN

INSIDE the cab of Esmerelda, his beloved three-
ton truck, Jefferson Crepe adjusted his wrap-
round sunglasses and shoved another piece of
chewing gum into his thin-lipped mouth. He
swept back his greased black hair with his
fingers, and turned up the volume of his heavy
rock music so loud that his shark tooth pendant
vibrated around his neck.

The Flyman

It was a trip he did four times a day, delivering fresh meat from the abattoir on the other side of Nab Top to his father's butcher's shop in Pearlbury. He knew the road like the back of his hand, every twist and turn, every bump, every pothole. It was a boring job but then Jefferson had never been very bright. At school, the only thing he'd been any good at was being the school bully. He'd blackmailed other kids to do his homework for him, and anyone who dared to turn him down paid for it – painfully. Even the teachers were too frightened to challenge him to work harder.

In the end, it was no surprise that Jefferson had ended up with a dead-end job, but he had ways of making his daily routine more interesting. Etched across his dashboard were dozens of

penknife notches, all part of a deadly game
Jefferson played to spice up his otherwise dull,
meaningless life. The notches were for each
"critter" he had run over.

"Yahoo! Here we go," he yelled as he spied
something up ahead. "You're mine, baby.
History. Dead meat."

The muscles on his tattooed arms bulged as he
gleefully tightened his grip on the steering wheel.
He turned the music up even louder, honked his
horn, changed gear and put his foot down hard
on the accelerator. Esmerelda growled an initial
protest before obediently surging forward,
burning up the bypass so fast that a smell of
rubber polluted the air and the thunderous noise
drowned out the desperate warning cries of a bird
from above.

The Flyman

SNOWDROP had reached the half-way point across the bypass, still in a biscuit-induced trance. He snapped out of it in a terrifying instant in which his blood froze.

The world was suddenly filled with an almighty rumble. Loose stones on the great concrete river were bouncing up and down like fleas. Overhead, Godric was circling, wildly, like an out of control kite in a squall. Snowdrop knew immediately what was happening. It was him – the legendary, merciless Flyman. Word of his dastardly deeds had spread across the meadow. He was a killing machine.

Every instinct told Snowdrop to curl up into a ball and let the Gods decide his fate. That's what normal spikeshufflers would have done – hidden from the reality, denied the truth. But Snowdrop

SNOWDROP

Hawthorn was no ordinary spikeshuffler. Far from it. Instead of burying his head and hoping the nightmare would go away, he began to run. He ran for dear life.

~

JEFFERSON Crepe had never seen anything like it. A hedgehog that was white, and one that could run! Not in all his years of driving his truck along Merlin's Highway had he been quite so excited. And, boy, could that critter move!

"Go girl. Go!" he yelled, coaxing yet more effort out of Esmerelda. "We got him, baby, we got him."

The truck hurtled onwards. The world was a blur. The grasses and wildflowers by the side of the road were laid flat, cowering in deference to such power. Even if the brakes had been slammed on now, it would take 100 yards to stop. But stopping was the last thing on Jefferson Crepe's mind. His penknife was waiting in the glove compartment. He wanted one more kill. One more notch on his dashboard. In fact, a rare albino would be worth more than one notch.

He was going to have to lurch on to the hard shoulder to stop his target getting away but that was OK. There was no-one around to see, apart from the old woman in the cottage and who cared about that stupid old bat?

"Yee-har! Come on Esmerelda, baby. That's my girl."

The roar of the engine was deafening. The screech of the tyres, as they swung towards

SNOWDROP

Snowdrop, was truly petrifying. The spikeshuffler, his heart pumping, could feel the truck's heat and smell the sickening combination of diesel and hot rubber...

~

IT was a smell so many of the Hawthorns had smelled in their last moments on this earth before they were squashed to a pulp: Willow Hawthorn, Stick Hawthorn, Bog Hawthorn, Brush Hawthorn, Daisy Hawthorn, Rose Hawthorn, Hyacinth Hawthorn, and Scrub Hawthorn.

These were only the victims of the year just past and, one by one, news of their deaths had reached Snowdrop through the animal grapevine. Each killing had brought fresh bouts of grief but the most recent had left the little white spikeshuffler utterly heartbroken. It was Godric who had told him in the gentlest voice, almost a whisper, one morning – a morning that Snowdrop would never forget as long as he lived.

"I'm sorry that it is me who must tell you," the great bird had said.

It was still so hard to believe but The Flyman had taken the great Twig Hawthorn, Snowdrop's dear father. Godric wasn't used to emotion. As a bird of prey, he knew death well – it was the way of the world. Life was gone in the flap of a wing and yet this was the hardest thing he had ever had to do. Snowdrop cried so much he thought he might never stop. There were enough tears to have filled The Great Pond.

It was no good. Snowdrop was fast but he wasn't quite fast enough. He realised that he wasn't going to make it. His stupid, stumpy little legs had failed him this time. Biscuits. All because of biscuits. But at least he hadn't curled up and surrendered.

As the final seconds of his life counted down, he turned to face his destiny. He would die with defiance in his soul – with his spikes upright and proud. The truck – hissing, smoking, squealing, shuddering – was almost upon him. Snowdrop looked up and caught a glimpse of him peering down through the windscreen. Frozen in time, he saw the sunglasses that made him look like a giant fly. He saw his fist raised in triumph. He saw his evil smile. He saw death in a monstrous pile of gleaming metal.

The Flyman

Snowdrop Hawthorn closed his eyes, knowing he would never open them again on the lush, vivid greenery of Merlin's Meadow. There was a final blaring of a horn, a dazzling shower of sparks, and a crescendo as loud as all the thunderclaps of a lifetime brought together in one cataclysmic storm. Then there was nothing. Silence. When Snowdrop opened his eyes, he had gone to heaven.

CHAPTER SIX

HEAVEN

SNOWDROP

HEAVEN was blue. Blindingly blue. So astonishingly blue that it brought tears to his eyes. Heaven also had fresh, pure air. After the diesel and the rubber, it was like drinking ice cold water to quench a terrible thirst. He couldn't catch hold of his thoughts but Snowdrop felt an exhilarating sense of freedom rushing through his body. Death wasn't something to be feared after all. It was a release. It was like his dream. It was like flying.

"Don't worry. You're safe," said a voice.

Snowdrop gasped. He wasn't alone. Was God talking to him? He tried to reply but couldn't. The wind wouldn't let him. Heaven was taking quite a bit of getting used to.

Snowdrop looked up through a mist of tears to see a pair of wings stroking, then gliding, stroking then gliding, stroking then gliding. An angel? It must be an angel sent to take him to God. Soon, he would meet God. And, perhaps, Twig, his dear father, and his dead brothers, sisters and cousins would be waiting for him too.

SNOWDROP

JEFFERSON Crepe banged the steering wheel with his fists in fury.

"How'd we miss?" he yelled.

There had been no familiar, satisfying squelch as Esmerelda's wheels had gone over the hedgehog. There was no flattened little body to be seen in his wing-mirror. One second, the critter had been his for the taking. It had given up trying to run. It was right there on the hard shoulder, ready for squashing. The next moment, there had been a flash of some kind and he was gone.

"How'd we miss, Esmerelda?" he repeated. "Where'd he go?"

Jefferson pulled over into a lay-by and walked back along the bypass towards Mrs Gibbons' cottage. The tyre marks veering onto the hard

shoulder were there but that was all. No
hedgehog pancake. Jefferson scratched his head
and trudged back to the truck. He took his
penknife out of the glove compartment, ran his
finger along the blade and drew blood in
frustration. There was to be no new notch on the
dashboard this time and it left him in a blinding
rage all the way to Pearlbury.

~

"DON'T think this makes us best friends because
it doesn't," said the voice.

Best friends? Why should Snowdrop expect to be
an angel's best friend? He couldn't even be
Godric's best friend because the space between
the earth and the sky was too great, so what

chance was there of befriending an angel?

Godric! The truth hit Snowdrop like a bolt from the blue. He wasn't in heaven. He wasn't being carried to God by an angel. But he *was* flying! He was flying with Godric!

"I wouldn't do this for anyone, you know," said Godric, calmly, his claws wrapped around the little spikeshuffler.

Snowdrop still couldn't find any words. Beneath him he could now make out the green patchwork of Merlin's Meadow. He could see the river running beside it, looking no bigger than a grass snake. And he could see so much more than he'd ever seen before: bright yellow cornfields to the east; swathes of shocking red poppies to the west; a collection of white-painted houses to the north; and a shimmering green sea to the south.

Heaven

His mother had told him stories of the sea – "a never-ending pond" – but he'd never quite known if they were true or just fairytales.

Suddenly, they were cartwheeling and looping so that the excitement was almost too much to contain. Snowdrop felt that he'd left his belly behind as they dived towards the river, then straightened out at the last second so that he skimmed the water with his stumpy, inadequate little legs.

"Yippeeeeeeeeee," shrieked Snowdrop, joyfully finding his voice at last. Seconds later they were rocketing skywards again. Up, up, up into the blue, blue nothingness. Incredibly, Nab Top was below them as they danced on invisible currents. They were higher than the highest mountain and, while he was still marvelling at the thought, Snowdrop found himself brushing through the snow that lay at its peak. In an instant they were back down to earth. Snowdrop was gently deposited on to a soft tuft of meadow grass and Godric flopped down beside him.

"That was amaaaaaaaaaaaaaazing!" gushed Snowdrop. "Better than any dream. I thought I was dead. I thought I was in heaven. I thought you were an angel taking me to God."

Having been unable to find any words, they were suddenly tumbling out of Snowdrop like rapids rushing towards a waterfall.

"What happened?"

"I tried to warn you," the windseeker explained. "The Flyman and his machine were almost upon you but I couldn't watch you die."

At the very last second, flying as swiftly as an arrow, he had grabbed the spikeshuffler in his claws and swept him to safety. It had been a close call. So close that Godric had lost a tail feather in the rescue.

"I was rather attached to that feather," sighed Godric, wistfully.

"You saved my life," whispered Snowdrop. "Thank you."

"When the difference between feast or famine depends on catching greyflappers, you develop a split-second sense of timing," boasted Godric. "Call me your guardian angel."

And, with that, he was gone in a flurry of feathers.

CHAPTER SEVEN

THE DREAM

SNOWDROP

DEEP inside his thicket, Snowdrop hardly slept that night. His mind was more active than ever, flickering between two main thoughts – the precious memories of his first flight, and the growing hatred he felt for The Flyman.

Snowdrop had always known in his heart that the deaths of his family and friends had been more than mere accidents. Now, his close encounter with The Flyman had confirmed it. There was only one word for it – he was a murderer.

"Honourable spikeshufflers, all of them," he thought to himself. "All killed for no good reason."

When he finally fell asleep, he dreamed deeply. He was a windseeker, cutting through the sky, and his blood coursed through his body with excitement all over again. He flew so high, he touched the sun. He flew so low, he splashed through water. He flew so long, he travelled the length of a rainbow.

Then, all too soon, it was over. He was back on solid ground. In fact, he was underground, in a pitch-black burrow. A light appeared at the end of the tunnel and he crawled towards it. As he got closer to the flame, he thought he saw a face – a familiar, ghostly face. Could it be true?

"Father?" he whispered. "My father?"

"My son," came the reply.

Tears flowed as Snowdrop nuzzled Twig Hawthorn. The colour had gone from Twig's body. He resembled an albino but it was unmistakably him. For several seconds, they said nothing. Just to be together again was enough.

Then Twig spoke.

"Listen. I cannot stay for long – the Gods are calling," he said. "There is little time, Snowdrop. It is up to you to stop it. Only you can stop the killings. The answer is on high. The answer is there – at the very top of the mountain."

The flame went out and Snowdrop instantly felt a stark, damp, cold loneliness.

"Father," he called. "Father, where are you?"

But no words came back. Twig Hawthorn had dissolved into the darkness. For a second time, he had disappeared.

THE days passed in a sad haze for Snowdrop. He
wanted – needed – to be alone so he walked and
walked until he found himself at the foot of Nab
Top Mountain. It was further than he'd ever been
before and the journey left him cold and tired.

The questions wouldn't stop. They hammered
away at his head like a hungry, determined

woodpecker at the bark of a great oak: Had his father really appeared to him from the other side? Or had it been a dream? What could his father have meant? What was he trying to say? The answer? On high? At the very top of the mountain? What could it be?

Snowdrop's pink eyes gazed up at the mountain peak, trying to work it out. It was hard to believe that he had soared even higher during his flight with Godric. At that moment, the windseeker came into view, appearing out of a cloud as a tiny speck, circling the snow-capped tip of the great mountain. Soon, it would be winter and the whole mountain would be white – albino. Soon, it would be time for the animals of Merlin's Meadow to slow down and for many of them to prepare for the big sleep. But Snowdrop must not stop. Not until he had found the answer.

"I need you, Godric," he found himself calling. "I need you."

CHAPTER EIGHT

DESTINY

SNOWDROP

JEFFERSON Crepe didn't like the winter much. He still had to drive Esmerelda back and forth through the valley, but it wasn't as interesting. There were never as many animals to target. The meadow seemed to grind to a halt and he had to drive a little slower to avoid the lorry sliding on the frozen roads. While he might average 10 penknife notches a week during high summer, he was lucky to get one a week – maybe a squirrel forced out through hunger – once the snow came.

Today, he was loading up Esmerelda with logs for a trip from Pearlbury to the coast, where they would be loaded onto a cargo ship. It was a favour for a friend of his father's who was a timber merchant. Who cared? It was work. Meat or wood, it made no difference. The drive to the coast still took him through Merlin's Meadow and there was always a chance to have some fun, even if it had been in short supply lately.

~

SNOWDROP didn't know how long he'd slept but, when he woke, Godric was waiting, perched on a low branch, dusted with snow, with his head tucked behind a wing to protect himself from the wind.

"You are troubled," said the windseeker, softly. "This is a long way from your home."
Snowdrop tried to gather his thoughts but they were as jumbled and confusing as the snowflakes that were falling.

"I need to fly again," he found himself saying.

"Why?" replied Godric. "What would be achieved? You are a spikeshuffler and spikeshufflers don't fly."

"I don't know. I just know that I must," Snowdrop whispered.

Godric asked no more questions. He fluttered down from his branch and lightly picked up the little spikeshuffler in talons that could easily have torn him apart. In an instant, they were skimming the hedgerows and skirting the trees on an ascent of discovery.

Soon, there was nothing; just a heavy, grey sky so different from the brilliant blue which had greeted Snowdrop's maiden flight. Snow swirled all around him in mesmerising patterns.

"Higher, higher," shouted Snowdrop. "I must go higher."

Destiny

Something inside him, deep within his soul, was urging him on. Godric responded by arching his wings to gather more air and flying upwards. And then the wind found a voice: "The answer is there – at the top of a mountain."

It was almost as if Godric had heard the voice too because he was circling Nab Top and came in to land on a snowy crag of rock which jutted out at right-angles from the peak.

"This is it. You must leave me here," said Snowdrop.

"But you will perish," replied Godric.

"If I am to die, then this is the place for it, high in the sky, up among the clouds and the wind," Snowdrop sighed. He looked up at his saviour of more than once. "Friends?" he asked.

SNOWDROP

The old windseeker looked down at Snowdrop and seconds passed in silence.

"Friends."

Destiny

GODRIC had vanished in two heavy, sombre beats of his wings and Snowdrop was alone, wondering what he – a mere spikeshuffler – was doing as the top of a mountain in the middle of a blizzard.

He knew he could not survive for long and he could already feel an aching numbness creeping up his legs and into his freezing body. Through the snowflakes, the sky was the colour of a shoal of greyflappers and the wind was as loud as The Flyman's mighty engine up close. Snowdrop stood there, hypnotised by the ever-changing white dotted patterns against the dark sky, and he felt a powerful urge to sleep. Once he was asleep, the pain would be gone, and he would never wake up. He would be with his father again.

His father. The thought jolted him back to

consciousness and the snowflakes began to swirl into circles, scurrying, flurrying, hurrying, like a million dandelion heads trapped in a whirlwind. When the swirling stopped, Snowdrop could make out a shape, just as his mother had taught him to see animals mapped out in the stars. It was a face, a strong, reassuring face – the face of his father.

Snowdrop was too cold to say a word but the voice of his father could be heard echoing on the wind.

"The time is now, my special son. "It is time to fly, time to fly, time to fly…"

The swirling began again and the face was gone. Snowdrop knew there was not a second left. He drew on what remained of his strength, forced himself to the very edge of the outcrop of rock, closed his eyes – and jumped.

CHAPTER NINE

REVENGE

SNOWDROP

JEFFERSON Crepe sat in Esmerelda's cabin with the door open. He was using his penknife on his thumb to pick out a splinter from one of the logs he had loaded. It was deeper than he thought and the blade drew blood as he cut underneath the black sliver of wood until one end poked up above the skin and he could pull it out with his teeth.

He put the penknife away, swung his legs inside the cab, pushed on his sunglasses to protect his eyes from the glare of the snow, and turned the key in the ignition. Esmerelda coughed and spluttered but didn't spark up. Jefferson cursed the cold and tried again. This time, the truck wheezed and whined, as if she were reluctant to embark on this latest journey. It took four attempts before she finally shuddered into life and that had never happened before.

"What's the matter with you, girl?" hollered Jefferson above the din. "It aint like you, that's for sure."

In truth, he wasn't relishing the trip too much either. There was something strange in the air, and he didn't just mean the snow. All the way across to the coast on a day like this, he groaned to himself. It might have been a blast on a hot summer's day, assassinating one or two critters on the road past Merlin's Meadow, with the promise of a nice cool beer at the other end. However, there wasn't much to look forward to on a day like this. Nope, it just didn't seem right.

SNOWDROP

SNOWDROP found himself lost in a world that was spinning and blinding white. Not for the first time in his relatively short life, he wondered if this was death. But this was nothing like he'd experienced before. It wasn't like flying. It was absolutely terrifying. He was now inside a white cocoon, rolling, over and over and over again. One second he was the right way up and the next he was upside down.

Revenge

From the air above, Godric was watching the most incredible spectacle. His friend, the spikeshuffler, had thrown himself from the top of the mountain, landed in the snow, and was now rolling down the slope inside a snowball that was getting bigger and bigger with every revolution. From the mountain peak, the snowball had left a track that had grown from spikeshuffler-size to cow-size within just a few seconds. It rolled, bounced and skidded, gathering speed and picking up rocks and small trees which were in its path. By the time it was a quarter of the way down the mountain, the snowball was already a hundred times the size of the little creature rolling around in an icy air pocket deep inside. To begin with, Snowdrop had never felt so dizzy but he was starting to get used to the ride. He had

managed to spread his legs so that his claws were jammed against the sides of the air pocket. He was still turning over and over but he wasn't being thrown around in quite the same heart-stopping way as before. In fact, it was starting to be fun, in a crazy, spike-tingling kind of way.

~

THE Flyman was bored out of his simple skull and in an irritable mood. Esmerelda was thundering along, maybe a mile or so from Merlin's Meadow, although something still wasn't quite right. She kept spluttering, throatily, and three times since they'd left Pearlbury, her brakes had engaged without warning with Jefferson Crepe having to pull her out of the resultant swerve.

"What's wrong with you?" he groaned through gritted teeth. "We gotta get you into the garage for a checkover when we get back. You're like an old woman with colic."

SNOWDROP

THE human known as The Whistler was busy cooking a handsome, juicy fish inside his neat log cabin halfway up Nab Top Mountain. He'd had a particularly fruitful morning on the river and he found nothing quite as satisfying as catching his own lunch. This one had put up a good fight, nearly got away, but was sure to taste good with some boiled potatoes and green beans.

There was a fine smell coming from the oven as he looked out of his window, whistling happily. The snow was still coming down good and hard and he was glad he had a healthy fire flaming in the grate.

At first, he thought the rumble was a low-flying aircraft, though there weren't many of those in these parts. As it grew louder, he started to wonder if Merlin's Meadow was about to be hit by an earthquake or tornado. Then he saw it. Coming over the crest of the hill was a snowball the size of a house. For a second, he thought his log cabin might be smashed into a pile of matchsticks but the snowball took a huge bounce, clearing the roof, and rolling on its way.

SNOWDROP

ETHEL Gibbons felt sorry for the animals in this weather. She'd left out some biscuits, bread and other tidbits as usual but she was particularly worried about the birds which hadn't flown south. It must be hard for them to get through these winter months, she thought to herself, so she emptied a bag of raisins onto the bird table and hung a few strings of peanuts from the washing line. That should keep them going.

Revenge

RUFUS Willow, the brushtail, stirred in his cosy nest high up in the trunk of a majestic pine. He didn't want to have to go out, not in this weather, but he was hungry. He couldn't believe how quickly his stock of nuts and berries had dwindled.

He peeped outside and didn't like the look of the falling snow but he'd be back as quickly as he could. He checked overhead. Nothing. He looked left and right. Nothing. So he scampered headfirst down the tree trunk and began foraging around the forest floor. He knew he needed to be especially careful because, as the last of the Merlin's Meadow red squirrels, his fur was worryingly bright against the whiteness all around him.

"Keep moving, keep moving – that's the trick,"

SNOWDROP

Rufus muttered to himself as he danced across the meadow, using the cover of the trees wherever he could, desperately hoping to come across some meaningful food. He'd already strayed further than he'd wanted to from the nest. The closer he could stay to the pine, the easier it would be all round because he could bury his findings in a place which was within easy reach the next time he felt hungry. But there was an unmistakeable, irresistible smell of peanuts in the air and he was following it as surely as a stream flows downhill. He found himself hunched on the wooden fence that marked the end of the meadow, looking across the road to the gardens on the other side. That was where the smell was coming from and he'd had rich pickings across there before.

Revenge

THE Flyman had reached his favourite stretch of road on the outskirts of Merlin's Meadow and, even on a day like this, it hadn't let him down. He couldn't believe his luck. He hadn't expected any fun at all on a day like this but, if he wasn't mistaken, there was a prize up ahead that was worth at least three penknife notches. A squirrel had jumped down from the fence and gingerly

taken its first step onto the bypass. Not an ordinary grey squirrel but a red one – and he hadn't seen one of those in these parts for years.

"Yahoody, yahoody," Jefferson Crepe shouted as he leaned forward, peering through the windscreen wipers, and squeezing the accelerator as much as he dare.

The red squirrel had taken two small hops and stopped to smell the air, forgetting his own advice to keep moving, keep moving, keep moving.

"We's gonna get him Esmerelda, we's gonna get him," chuckled Jefferson, excitedly.

Like so many others before him, Rufus Willow heard the grinding and screaming of the engine too late. He turned to see the murderous truck was almost upon him and his whole body went rigid with horror. The air was filled with deafening noise as the world seemed to go into slow-motion. Stones, thrown up from Esmerelda's tyres, pinged around liked bullets, a horn was blaring randomly, heavy rock music throbbing, and the wagon's headlights shone through the gloom like a pair of wicked orange eyes.

The Flyman was cackling, manically, inside his cab as he went in for the kill but the laughing stopped in an instant and was replaced with a disbelieving "Ugh?".

What in heaven's name was that, heading his way, bowling uncontrollably across the meadow at the kind of speed a truck could never reach? Jefferson Crepe began to cry and wet his pants as the giant juggernaut of a snowball smashed through the wooden fence, missing the petrified Rufus Willow by a whisker. There was a blood-curdling screech of brakes, a muffled scream, and then an ear-splitting impact which made the earth shake and send a thousand frightened birds exploding into the air.

As big and strong as Esmerelda was, she was crushed like a flimsy tin can. The snowball rolled on a little way up the road before finally coming to a halt and breaking in half, like a hatching egg. A nervous white snout, with an icicle hanging from the end, poked out, followed by a pair of redcurrant eyes which took time to find their focus. When they did, Snowdrop could hardly believe what he saw. It was a scene of devastation: the mangled, pancake-flat wreckage, steaming on the tarmac; a pair of trademark sunglasses cracked and twisted by the side of the road; and a red brushtail darting back into the undergrowth.

The little spikeshuffler looked across to the beautiful, snow-covered outline of Nab Top. He could make out the ever-widening grey scar that had been gouged down the mountainside and it didn't take long for him to understand what had happened. It was what he, Snowdrop the albino spikeshuffler, the freak of nature, had been born for. The Flyman had made his last penknife notch on his dashboard and the lost souls of Merlin's Meadow could finally rest in peace.

Snowdrop sighed, contentedly, as he began the walk home, and the triumphant cries of a windseeker in the sky above lifted the spirits of every creature for miles around.

CHAPTER TEN

TIME PASSES

SNOWDROP

A LITTLE white van chugged its way, carefully, through the valley, the driver humming to himself as the autumn sunshine flickered through the yellow and orange leaves of the roadside trees, making kaleidoscopic patterns on his face.

Beside him on the passenger seat was a small cage. Inside was a young hedgehog, which had found it hard to live in the wild and was in need of some tender loving care before winter began to bite. He'd never seen a hedgehog with a peculiar, single white spike on its back before.

"We'll soon have you somewhere safe, little buddy," said the driver, softly. "Don't you worry about nuttin' – d'ya hear?"

The driver, a dark-haired man with a few flecks of grey, swallowed hard as he passed the spot where he'd so nearly been killed on that fateful day too many years ago. He didn't like to talk about it too much but some kind of avalanche had come down from Nab Top mountain and crushed his wagon. Even now, he wasn't sure how he'd survived. Just as the snow had hit, he'd flung open his cab door and thrown himself out on to the road. He'd rolled down a hill and into some bushes. It was days before they found him and, when he woke up, fixed to wires in a hospital bed, they told him he'd been unconscious for nigh on four weeks. They'd given up on him more than once, said the nurses, so he'd better thank his lucky stars.

As he slowly recovered, the world began to seem a different place to Jefferson Crepe. By the time he was finally allowed to leave hospital with the help of crutches, he felt very different

too. A blackbird hopped in front of him on the path out of the hospital grounds and he found himself standing still so that it wouldn't be frightened. When it flew off, he watched it go, marvelling at its beauty and sharing its sense of joy at being alive and free.

A short while afterwards, when his legs had healed and the crutches weren't needed anymore, he'd started working as a volunteer at the Pearlbury Animal Rescue Centre. He'd never enjoyed anything so much: helping to treat injured animals, cleaning out the pens and cages, dishing up the food, and driving round the valley to pick up all kinds of critters that had been reported to be hurt or trapped.

A woman, out walking her dog, had come across the little hedgehog now riding along with him in his van. When she phoned in, the woman swore she'd seen an eagle swoop down and leave the animal on the track in front of her, then circle overheard until she'd picked it up and wrapped it in a handkerchief. Jefferson smiled at the thought. He'd never heard anything so far-fetched in all his cotton-pickin' life. What he did know was that the little hedgehog with the white spike was so sick and exhausted, the poor little mite wouldn't have lasted another hour out in the meadow on his own.

"Here you go, little fella," said Jefferson as he pulled up outside the rescue centre, cradled the cage in both hands, and walked inside to deliver the animal to a waiting vet.

SNOWDROP

OH, how contented old Snowdrop Hawthorn would have been to know that his legacy lived on and that another member of the family – another descendant in the great line of Hawthorns – was being well cared for in its hour of need.

Many summers had passed since he'd left the earth to go to a new world up in the clouds, but he hadn't been forgotten. Certainly not. Across Merlin's Meadow, they still talked of the legend of the pure white spikeshuffler.

At night-time, all kinds of animals told their offspring epic stories of his bravery and how he'd lived to be the oldest, wisest – and fastest – spikeshuffler ever known.

Time passes

They told how, from the moment his eyes had blinked open, next to his dear mother and father in the old hedgerow, Snowdrop Hawthorn had been different. Right from the beginning, he'd been...special.

THE END

THE ILLUSTRATOR

Just like Snowdrop the Spikeshuffler, Jonathan Raiseborough found it hard when he was growing up... because he was different.

He was born with a condition called Asperger's syndrome, which is on the autism spectrum. It made social interaction difficult for Jonathan. He struggled to make friends and, at times, he was bullied.

But, again like Snowdrop the Spikeshuffler, Jonathan isn't just different – he's special. As you can see from this book, he has a special talent.

Jonathan is 18 now and lives in Darlington, where he is studying art at college. His gift for drawing has helped him to overcome the difficulties he faced as a little boy. It has given him confidence and belief in himself.

When he was growing up, he dreamed of being an illustrator of children's books. Snowdrop The Spikeshuffler marks his debut as a professional illustrator.

THE AUTHOR

Peter Barron is an established author of children's books as well as an award-winning journalist.

He was editor of The Northern Echo for 17 years and also edited the Hartlepool Mail. He is a former UK Columnist of the Year and was awarded the MBE for services to journalism.

He has so far had seven children's books published in the Monstrous Morals series: Fartin' Martin Sidebottom, Black-toothed Ruth Black, Fidgety Bridget Wrigglesworth, Messy Bessie Clutterbuck, Nose-picking Nicholas Pickering, Daydreaming Daisy McCloud, and Chilly Billy Winters.

The stories help to get across the message about children's bad habits, and there are more to come. Snowdrop was inspired by a press cutting from The Northern Echo about a real-life albino hedgehog which had been taken to an animal sanctuary because he was being picked on in the wild.

THE NORTH EAST AUTISM SOCIETY

When Peter met Jonathan by chance, and heard about his ambitions to be an illustrator of children's books, he wanted to encourage him so he sent him the unpublished manuscript of Snowdrop the Spikeshuffler.

To Peter's surprise and delight, Jonathan responded by producing the first samples of the beautiful illustrations you now see in this book.

This story, about overcoming prejudice, has been turned into a book with the generous support of the North East Autism Society, a pioneering organisation which cares for people with autism in Jonathan's home region.

Between one and two per cent of the population has some level of autism and one of the society's key objectives is to help more people with autism to find employment.

Jonathan's CV has been enriched. He is on his way.

He's flying.

And the message is very simple: Don't judge someone just because they are different.